HUMMING
Whispers

Also by Angela Johnson

Toning the Sweep

HUMMING
Whispers

Angela Johnson

ORCHARD BOOKS

ORCHARD BOOKS
96 Leonard Street, London EC2A 4RH
Orchard Books Australia
14 Mars Road, Lane Cove, NSW 2066
ISBN 1 86039 214 8 (hardback)
ISBN 1 86039 099 4 (trade paperback)
Originally published in the United States in 1995
by Orchard Books, New York
First published in Great Britain in 1996
First paperback publication 1996
Copyright © Angela Johnson 1995
A CIP catalogue record for this book is available
from the British Library.
Printed in Great Britain by The Guernsey Press Ltd

To Sandy Perlman,
who knows the way

Part One

1

I GOT LOST in a store once when I was four. I remember it all so clear now. I remember how soft the nightgowns felt as I turned around in them while they hung on the rack. I remember how the popcorn smelled as I watched a boy in a blue cap scoop it all up in tall white bags. I remember Aunt Shirley's perfume and her warm sweater as I buried my head against her chest.

My sister, Nicole, has figured out the day I got lost was the first time she heard the whispers. She'd wandered away from the store, leaving Aunt Shirley to call and call for her. Other people started calling as she stood in the middle of traffic in the parking lot. Aunt Shirley ran after her, forgetting about me. Nicole was fourteen.

We didn't know it then, but they'd stay with us. The whispers.

They hang in the air around us, even though sometimes they're quiet for days, even months. Nikki says other times they're hissing whispers that chase her through the apartment and out the door. Or they're humming whispers like the ones she followed into the parking lot the day I danced in the soft nightgowns in the women's department.

She's staring out the front window now, waiting for Them. She won't tell me or Aunt Shirley who Them is. We only ask once, then sit together for a while in the wicker chairs, watching the sun pour through.

We all want to believe Them have gone for ever, but they're not gone. They've hung around for ten years. They'll always be with us, like the birthmarks on our bodies; changing maybe, but never really going away.

Aunt Shirley says the sun shines on, though, and it just is. We get up expecting it to shine brighter some days than others. We never get up expecting it not to be there. Aunt Shirley's way of saying, "Live with it." And we do.

2

FROM THE ROOF of my school the world looks calm. Everything's in order. Rows of everything. Nothing's crazy way up here. It's all clear. I like the view from the roof.

I come to the roof instead of going to independent study. In the beginning I used to dance up here. I'd dance like a fool, 'cause there was nothing else I wanted to do as much.

Nicole is a secret dancer, but only when she's sick. When she isn't, she dances around the apartment whenever the mood hits her. Or she joins in with me, clapping as I fly across the floor. Her steps are mine; we both know the other's moves before we make them.

I know when my sister is sick she wants to dance.

5

I can tell by her legs. I think they're trying to dance their way out of the whispers. Step. Step. Dance. The steps won't come, though.

They'd let her dance at City Hospital if she wanted to. They'd let her dance to any music at all. It's just that she can't do it.

Nicole used to come to the roof when she went to school here. She'd watch the planes. I'm afraid of them. Have nightmares about 'em, too. But, yeah, everything else is okay up here.

TODAY NICOLE takes me to her place by the airport. We've come here before. We lie on the grass and let the planes fly over us. They're so close, our whole world trembles as they pass.

Nicole screams to me over the jets. "Can you hear it, Sophy?"

"Yeah," I holler back.

"I mean, can you really hear it? Can you hear the clicking in the engine and the wheels folding up into the belly?"

I look over at my sister and she's beautiful. Always has been. But she's never so beautiful as she is when her eyes flash. They do now.

"I hear it, Nikki. I do. I really do," I yell at her.

"That's what's important, you know? That you hear it all. You have to hear it all."

Nikki sits up and stretches. The plane has gone on, and we wait for the next one. Her white pants are grass-stained, but it won't do me any good to tell her about it. Nikki doesn't care about the way she looks. She never really did; but after she got sick, it made her mad if someone mentioned it.

I move closer to my sister. I know she feels like going away from me. I feel it, but my closeness pulls her back.

I look around us at the blackberry bushes. A few weeks ago Nikki found a path through them. We still get scratched a little, but it's worth it, coming here. The leaves are starting.

"When's the next plane, Nikki?"

She always knows. She can hear them down the runway before they take off, before I ever hear them.

She throws herself back and screams, "Now!"

It's a game she always wins.

I hold on to my sister's hand as her eyes flash and the world is one big pocket of sound with only us in it.

AUNT SHIRLEY'S been waiting for us. I can tell from way down the avenue 'cause of how she gets up off the stoop when she sees us coming. It's like she's been caught. Caught worrying about us. She doesn't know that I know she worries.

The bus we just got off passes us by, and I see

Aunt Shirley wave to somebody on it before she turns to go in. It makes me feel good to see her wave. She always waves to me and Nicole when we leave the building. Makes me feel warm. She's always done it.

Maybe she waved to our parents the day they went off to that concert and never came back. Aunt Shirley says their car crash was the reason she gave up driving. Afterwards, she took Nicole and me and moved to the city, where there are buses and taxis. She told us that her brother, our daddy, might have been sad at the thought of no backyard for us, but she couldn't drive any more. Couldn't bear it.

We cross the avenue and in a few seconds are in our apartment. Fourth floor, last one on the right. It's the only place I can ever remember living. Aunt Shirley sits on the couch and nods to us. Nicole walks across the living room and settles on the floor beside her.

"We lay under the planes, Aunt Shirley. We did most of the day. Sophy loves the planes, too."

Aunt Shirley looks across the room at me and frowns. I look out the window and watch the birds on the ledge. The sun is starting to set. It doesn't feel like we've been gone most of the day.

"So how was it, Sophy?"

"How was what, Aunt Shirley?"

Aunt Shirley shifts around on the couch, and

Nicole smiles up at me. She winks, then stands up and walks into the kitchen.

Aunt Shirley clears her throat. "The planes, lil' sister. How were the planes?"

"They were fine, Aunt Shirley. She loves the planes."

"I know she does."

"I watch her, Aunt Shirley."

Aunt Shirley comes over to me. Her arms are cool as she wraps them around me. "You don't have to watch her now. I mean, she's all right now, sis."

"For now," I say.

Aunt Shirley rubs my shoulders, then goes in the kitchen after Nicole. I hear Nicole laughing at something that Aunt Shirley has said.

I love hearing Nikki laugh. Sometimes I do anything to get her going. I'll search through all the movie tapes underneath the TV, looking for something to make her laugh. Some nights we'll stay up all night long, just giggling. Nicole likes bad horror movies. She likes to throw popcorn at the screen.

Aunt Shirley says it's possibly therapeutic. I don't think so. Nikki just gets a kick out of tossing popcorn. She's more than a person who's sick, but sometimes Aunt Shirley can't see past that, can't see underneath.

It's my sister, Nicole, underneath the sickness, my sister who sings songs real loud in elevators and

9

rearranges the clothes on mannequins in stores. I know it. I know her. I know what she would be without the sickness and the medicine and the doctors. She'd be a twenty-four-year-old college graduate, instead of a twenty-four-year-old who takes classes while her medication is working.

Sister, sister. She's all the family I have – her and Aunt Shirley. And Reuben, I guess. I know I shouldn't be afraid for someone who can sing in elevators and speak three languages. I'm trying every day. I'm trying not to be afraid. That's all I have to remember. That's what I have to hold on to.

But it's hard not to be afraid when fear's been with you most of your life.

3

REUBEN HARDING got shot accidentally in the army, then sent home last year. He plays the saxophone and has the biggest collection of boots I've ever seen. He also loves my sister almost as much as Aunt Shirley and I do.

I sometimes wonder why he stays around. I've never met anybody like him. When Nicole's in the hospital, he's always there for Aunt Shirley and me. I don't think he's ever going to give up.

Nicole's doctors talk to him like family now. He'll get a call about her just as soon as Aunt Shirley will.

Once at the airport, while we lay on our backs, waiting for the next plane, Nikki said Reuben was "steadfast and true". She said poems used to be written about people like him.

She said she wanted to believe that if she were ever locked in a castle, she'd figure a way to get herself out. But if she were too weak from lack of food and her brains were gone, she figured Reuben would be the perfect person to get her out. He wouldn't brag about it or make her feel like she owed him anything. Then she rolled over to me and said, "But learn to get yourself out of locked castles," just as a plane roared overhead.

SOMETIMES, when all I have to do is sit around with my headset on, I look out the window and try to find my friends' houses. East Side and West Side. I've been all over the city. Reuben says most people haven't.

If you're born on the East Side, they think you have to buy everything there and die there, too. Same goes for the ones living on the West Side. I live in the city proper, so I can go any way, and I do.

The neighbourhood isn't so good, but there's always something to see. On one side of us is the Plasma Alliance, and on the other side, a big old mansion that some people are fixing up. I've been checking them out for a few days. They're not from around here. They call to the street people on the corner; they speak to everybody. I'm waiting. Careful, 'cause that's just the way it is.

*

I DO ALL KINDS of stuff for Aunt Shirley when she's at work. She has rules about being out in the streets, but I never need reminding. I learned them before I started school. Nicole had a harder time. She grew up in the country.

Yesterday, I went to the phone company after school and paid the bill. If it's on anybody's way and we don't have to use a stamp, Aunt Shirley says pay with your feet. She gets off work too late to do it herself. She says tofu is hell.

That's what she does. She makes tofu at this place in the warehouse district. She got the job when we first moved to the city.

Aunt Shirley says she used to keep a diary but stopped the year after she got out of high school and moved here. That was the year she spray-painted dye on baby seals so they wouldn't be killed for their pelts, started painting for real, and became our mother. By the end of the year she was making tofu.

Aunt Shirley says that she just couldn't think of anything else to put in the diary.

Real life was happening too strong, I guess.

I was thinking about starting one of my own. I even went into a Hallmark store at the mall. I shouldn't have tried to go in there around Valentine's Day, though. Everything smelled sweet, and there was so much pink and red I got confused. I ended up buying these big chocolate hearts for Aunt Shirley and Nicole. I bought about twelve cards and a helium balloon that said *Happy St Patrick's Day*.

Don't know what came over me. It could have been the boy behind the counter. He shouldn't smile at people the way he did.

So, no diary. I went into the grocery store once for dinner and came home with seven cans of green beans and four packs of hot-dog buns. When I got out on the street, I was too tired to go back in and wait in line again. A list is the way to go. We got 'em all over the apartment.

Lists for things to clean around the place.

Lists for clothes to take to the cleaners.

Lists for the maintenance man.

Lists of things for Nicole to remember.

Lists of things to remind me to remind Nicole of.

When I start complaining about the lists, Aunt Shirley laughs and says life is hard in the city.

4

THERE'S THIS BOY in school whose uncle was lost in the Great Lakes. The ship he was on just sank underneath all that water, and nobody really knows what happened. That was years before we were born. Now his uncle's only a name that comes up at family reunions and holidays. I guess the boy mentioned it 'cause we were talking about the Bermuda Triangle.

Some people think that there's a Great Lakes Triangle. Just doesn't sound right to me. I can see Lake Erie from our living-room window if I tiptoe and squint past two or three buildings that pretty much block most of the view. It's a friendly-looking lake. Now.

Not in the winter.

Or during a storm.

The storm time on the lake shakes me. The whole world might be tipping over.

Nicole likes storms on the lake. So does Aunt Shirley.

I just sit around, hoping that all the sailboats and speedboats are docked and the people who own them are dry and warm someplace. If I catch the weather on the news, I always want to run to the lake with a megaphone and scream to everybody to get back to shore. I want to invite 'em in for tea until the storm is over, 'cause some of 'em might think the same way Aunt Shirley and Nicole think and go out into the storm.

I've always wanted our own private basement during storms. To get to this building's basement takes about five minutes. The world could be blown away by that time. Anyway, we never go there during a storm. Aunt Shirley and Nicole watch the wind and lightning out our big leaded windows.

I sit on my bed with my storm suitcase beneath it.

It's always in the same place from April to September, sometimes October.

You can't be too careful. I mean, there's a weather channel now, a whole channel all by itself, like sports or news. I know that means something. We should take this stuff seriously.

Nicole only watches the weather to monitor plane

take-offs. If it looks too windy, she won't go. She says it's too hard to look straight up when the wind is blowing.

"YOU GOING to school today?"

Aunt Shirley stands at the door to our bedroom. Every morning she stands the same way, head tilted to the side, leaning against the door frame. She always asks the same question, too. She doesn't expect an answer.

I raise my hand to show her I'm awake; then she leaves.

I flip over to see if Nicole is awake yet. She sleeps in most mornings, but a few times a month she gets up and walks me to school. It's a change for her. I like her walking with me. Since she's ten years older than me, I never got to walk to school with her. She sleeps on today.

Last night the cops were all over the neighbourhood. I heard people running and doors slamming. I didn't get up to see who they were after, but I know Nicole was up watching. Since there was no shooting, they were probably after the women who stand on the corners at night and walk around the lobby of the apartment building across the street.

Our neighbour Earl across the hall calls them leisure women, but Aunt Shirley says they work. I know they do. They're just getting up when I'm coming home from school. I see them sitting on their tiny balconies in warm weather in robes, sipping coffee.

Nikki says that the women on the corner are the saddest people she knows of. They're even sadder than some of the people she's gotten to know at the hospital. Real sad.

She says I don't know sad, but I do. She can't understand how I'm sometimes sad for her, more than the women on the corner.

Nicole moves and is awake in a second.

"Did you hear them last night, lil' sis?"

"Mmm. You don't think anybody got arrested, do you?"

"I saw a couple people put in the back of the police cars."

I get up and go over to the window. The street is quiet every morning. "Nobody got hurt, did they?"

Nikki stares up at the ceiling and counts the fish up there. Aunt Shirley painted them a few years ago. They glow in the dark. Fish swimming across our ceiling.

Nikki says, "I guess not. I mean, not that I saw. I didn't want to have to call the station last night. I was so tired."

We call the police station anytime somebody gets hurt in a raid. The corner women shouldn't be knocked around in the raids, but sometimes they are. When they are, we call the station and say we're going to call the newspaper.

Aunt Shirley says even if you don't agree with what someone does, you shouldn't stand 'round watching them get hurt. If we watch out for them, it makes the world better; even if they don't return the favour.

I don't know if Nicole thinks about it that way, but I know she doesn't want people hurt.

It's too much sometimes. The people on the corner and at the blood bank. I wanted to move a couple of years ago, when this boy in our building got shot, but Aunt Shirley said she'd have to do more than make tofu and sell fish paintings to get us out of here.

It was worse that time 'cause Nicole was in the hospital then. I'd heard the shot and it echoed four flights up to our apartment, long after I was alone and the street was quiet.

TOAST FOR BREAKFAST and I'm outside before I know it. Garbage cans are turned over, and there's a striped scarf lying in the road. That's all that's left of last night. There's nothing else to let you know that anything happened in the dark.

After a couple of blocks I start seeing backpacks

and people riding bikes. I haven't found anybody on my block who goes to 36th Street School.

It's an art school. Performing and fine. While everybody else in the city is worrying about uniforms, kids at 36th bitch about how the performance artist should have been allowed to take her shirt off at the dance concert.

I can't think what other schools would be like. I've gone to university schools and got used to ten or fifteen students in a classroom all with paper and pencils, writing everything down and staring at me. 36th is easy. I'm ready for anything.

I am a dancer. Pure and true. Even when I was little, everybody knew it. My neck is long; and the dance is in me. That's what I study at 36th Street School.

If I'm standing somewhere waiting for the bus, I go to first position with my feet. I do it automatically. Once me and Paco started dancing right in the furniture department at Kaufmanns. We didn't even bump into a display. We were smooth. I'm a dancer. Everybody knows.

AS I GET CLOSER to the school, more and more people swarm around in groups. They smoke their last cigarettes and call to people across the street at the 7-Eleven.

I stand alone in a big crowd of people waiting to

go through the metal detectors at the door. No need to push anybody 'cause it's one by one.

Everybody seems to sleepwalk as the security guards say, "Keep it moving," and it looks to me like we're all lost in the Great Lakes.

5

I'M SITTING on Reuben's front stoop, waiting for him. He says he'll drive me over to the West Side Market. Nicole's birthday is tomorrow, and Aunt Shirley has said I should pick a few things up.

We don't celebrate our birthdays like most people do. Anyway, I don't think many people celebrate like us. We go to the cemetery and bring a lunch.

Since our parents are buried side by side, it's easy to hang out with them. We've been doing it for so long, I was surprised when some kids at school thought it was strange.

Paco told me that in Mexico there is a festival for the dead. I didn't feel so strange then. Aunt Shirley says that "we're just being in the presence" and leaves it at that.

REUBEN PULLS UP to the kerb in his pride and joy. He fixed up an old mail jeep and had it painted a deep dark green. He drives it everywhere. He says the jeep ran better than any car he'd ever had when him and Nicole went cross-country last year. Nicole says it was too small, but she'd miss it if he ever gave it up.

Reuben unfolds his legs out of the jeep. He's got on black cowboy boots today.

"You been waitin' long, sister?"

I go over to the jeep and help him unload big plastic bags of clay. He does pottery, throws pots on a wheel for the fun of it. Aunt Shirley and him took some ceramics classes at the community centre last winter.

I say, "Not too long. I walked over here from school."

"You mean that prison on Thirty-sixth?"

"It's not so bad. It's better than most."

Reuben unlocks the front door, and we drag everything in. He knocks on his neighbour's door. Miss Onyx Phelps is deaf so he knocks hard, then calls out, "I'm back, Miss Onyx."

A tiny old woman with bright red hair opens the door and smiles up at us. Reuben takes some papers out of his back jeans pocket and hands them to her.

"You should have gone with me to your lawyer's office, Miss Onyx. Lawyer says she misses you."

Miss Onyx smiles the brightest smile you've ever seen. She told me last year that she was ninety-two and had all her teeth – and her natural hair colour. When I asked Reuben if it was true, he said, "If she says so."

"That young girl is the best lawyer! She talks to me like I have some sense. She's about the tenth one I've had – and how are you, Sophy?"

"Just fine, Miss Onyx, and you?"

"Better than good, child, but it is time for my talk show."

Reuben walks on down the hall past the radiator and calls over his shoulder that he'll check on her later. I close Miss Onyx's door tight as she goes back in. I hear her television blaring down the hallway as I walk into Reuben's apartment. Reuben says it's not that she forgets to close the door; it's just that she's trusting.

Reuben's grandmother and Miss Onyx were best friends. When his grandmother died, he started looking after Miss Onyx. She wrote him twice a week without fail when he was in the army. He said she was always telling him that it was a sin to kill, and if they were about to make him kill somebody, he was to put his gun down.

I asked him if she'd meant it. He said, "She said it, didn't she?"

Reuben's apartment has nothing on its white walls except in the hallway. He's got a line of pencil drawings there. All of Nikki. He started doing them when she was sixteen, the year they met. They're all drawn on paper so creamy you want to touch it.

The rest of Reuben's place is bare. He says he can't stand clutter. Too much army, he says. All he has is plants and four big overstuffed chairs. I love his apartment better than ours; and he's a second from his basement.

"I'm gonna clean up a little, then we'll take off." He goes to his bedroom and turns on Screamin' Jay Hawkins.

He calls out, "Did Nikki go to her appointment?"

He knows I don't know and won't know until I get home, but I say yes anyway.

I yell down the hall to him, "She's doing a whole lot better, her best spring in a long time. I think the new medicine is working."

Reuben comes into the living room and gets his keys off the top of the stereo and says, "You think so?"

"Yeah, I think so – I said it, didn't I?"

Reuben is still laughing as we pull away in the jeep.

THE BEST PART of the market for me is all the people. I sometimes go just to watch them. It's another world at the market. I even see people from school there. I don't ever see them anywhere else.

At West Side you can hear six languages spoken in the span of fifty feet. Sometimes I just stand and close my eyes, taking it all in. The smells and the sounds.

Reuben stops at a vegetable stand, looking for seedless cucumbers. I've never heard of them, but he says Nicole loves them on salads. Whenever he talks about my sister, his voice lowers and sounds so sweet.

I walk over to Big Ray's Barbecue and order a rack of ribs. Big Ray is behind the counter.

He folds his arms across his chest. "You're Shirley's child, aren't you?"

I press my face against the glass, looking down at the ribs, and mumble, "Yes," then I stand up straight and say it louder.

I point to what I want, and Big Ray wraps it up for me.

"How's your sister? Doing better?"

He doesn't know us that well, so I know he's only asking out of politeness.

"She's fine. Got a birthday tomorrow. The ribs are for her."

"Birthdays are fine things," he says. "I've had a few myself."

I look at Big Ray's face and wonder how many. I

really can't tell and no way will I ask. Before Big Ray hands me the ribs, he wraps up another rack and puts a jar of his barbecue sauce in a bag for me. He puts it all in a plastic bag and says, "No charge," then turns his back and starts working at the chopping board in the corner.

I say thanks, but he waves me away.

I buy so many flowers with the money I still have that they barely fit in Reuben's jeep.

We drive through the city with the car smelling good and dripping with flowers, talkin' about how Nicole will love tomorrow. As Reuben's eyes shine, I think at that second maybe he loves my sister even more than Aunt Shirley and me.

More and different.

"DID YOU FIND my shoes, Sophy?"

I'm home from the market. Nicole comes out of our bedroom, rubbing her eyes. Her doctor had her in for a check-up today. She goes over to the Buddha on the table, picks him up, and looks underneath. For the last few days she's been keeping the new medication there. When I ask her why, she shrugs and asks me where I think she should put it.

"I saw Reuben. He was asking about you." I get up and look under the Buddha myself. "No. Nothing here," I tell Nikki.

"Hmph. Tell him I'm not seeing shoes under statues. At least not yet."

She has her hair in two thick plaits. Some hair still sticks out. It hasn't all grown back since she cut it off the winter before last. Nikki sinks down in her favourite chair. Earl and his room-mate, Paul, were going to throw the thing out. We rescued it from the garbage and painted big grey and red fish all over the tweedy cover. The fish on the ceiling of our bedroom inspired us.

I go over and sit on Nikki's lap. She swivels us around on the chair.

Nikki pulls a candy bar out of her shirt, breaks it in half, and hands me my part.

"You're too skinny, Sophy."

I pinch my thighs. "What can I do? I eat everything I can."

She hands me the rest of her chocolate. "You better pick up some weight. Even the school nurse thinks so, Aunt Shirley tells me. Well, I guess some people would want your problem."

"You know anybody who wants to be called Bones or Skeleton?"

Nicole swivels the chair around again.

"No, don't know anybody who'd like that. It's still all relative, I guess."

I eat all the chocolate and lick the rest off my hands.

"What does that mean – relative?"

"It means everybody has got something . . ."

"There're girls in my class killing themselves to drop five pounds. But I can't ever talk about my weight problem. Most of my friends don't see it as a problem."

"Most of them don't know what a problem is yet."

I guess my shoulders get stiff or something 'cause she takes it back.

"Sorry, girl. I know some of them have problems."

Nicole lifts me off her lap and starts back into the bedroom. On the way there she stoops and looks around. She's still looking for the pair of shoes she lost.

Lost things really bother her. Lost means she must not have been paying attention. If she wasn't paying attention to where she put her shoes, she worries about not paying attention to more important things.

Then the real worrying starts.

She'll start worrying that maybe she can't cross the street or that we've left the stove on in the apartment. She worries about the four long flights of stairs to the street – maybe she'll fall down them and nobody will hear her.

It starts like this sometimes.

It ends with shots and doctors and the apartment so quiet when I come home from school that I turn on every radio and the television at the same time.

The bad thing is we never really know. We've never been able to hit it just right 'cause sometimes the whispers come clear out of the blue. That's the hurting part.

Just when we think it's going to be okay.

Nicole dances into the living room. She's found her shoes and does a spin in the middle of the floor. She grabs me by the hands and we skip around, almost breaking the Buddha. I sit down beside the table and scoot him back to the centre.

I hear the key turn in the lock. As Aunt Shirley drops her purse on the floor and is closing the door, Nicole starts out of the room, smiling and humming.

Nicole whispers, "It's not schizophrenia this time, not this time," then shuts the bedroom door.

6

THEY KEEP day-old ham-
burgers at Doggy's
Restaurant and put 'em in the next morning's home
fries. Best in the city. You get your own coffee at
Doggy's, and if anybody else needs a refill while
you're up, you get some for them, too.

Today I sit next to two guys I recognize from
school. They wear their hats backward and their
sunglasses dark. One's growing an Afro and the other
has shaved his whole head.

They got off a West Side bus in front of Doggy's. I
listen to them talking about blowing off school today
to hang out at the art museum. Only kids from 36th
Street School would skip for that. I'm skipping to
hang out with my family at the cemetery.

A woman with bright purple hair gets on the

phone at the end of the counter and starts screaming at somebody named Steve. I take another bite of my home fries and listen to her side of the fight.

This always happens at Doggy's. I've heard some of the best phone fights anybody will ever hear. Doggy doesn't have a pay phone, but anybody can use his. He's got a block on it so you can't call long-distance. He says he hates hearing money fall into anything but his hands. So no pay phones at Doggy's, just a cup that everybody knows to drop a dime in. Calls are cheap at Doggy's.

I'm here 'cause on birthday mornings the apartment looks like a storm has blown through. Aunt Shirley leaves tofu early so she can get everything ready for the afternoon. From the looks of the sky, I'm thinking rain.

I can finish only half my food, so I shove it towards the boy growing the Afro.

He turns around on his stool. "You going to school today?"

I gulp down my orange juice and say, "No, I'm having a picnic with my parents at the cemetery."

He nods and eats a spoonful of Doggy's best home fries. There's even a sign outside that says, BEST HOME FRIES IN CLEVELAND. The woman with the purple hair is screaming at somebody named Tom as I walk out the door towards home.

*

I THINK I could find my way in this neighbourhood with my eyes closed. I wouldn't have any trouble crossing the streets either. It's like going from my bedroom to the kitchen. Familiar and everyday. I've been thinking about blindfolding myself and trying it.

They're lining up to give blood next door and the new people are still at it. Are they opening up a store or what?

A woman in jeans and a pink sweater waves to me and hands a lamp to one of the moving men to take inside.

After I run up the last flight of stairs, I can hear Reuben's saxophone music floating out the door. It's taped and we play it a lot. His music is all that Nicole will listen to in the morning. She says it's pure sweetness; then she wiggles her hips and acts like she's playing the sax herself.

Aunt Shirley pulls the red and green quilt from the back of the couch, folds it into a duffle bag, and drops the bag near the door.

"Where you been, sis?"

Nicole looks under the couch – probably for her shoes.

"She's been to Doggy's for breakfast," she says, looking up at me. "I can tell. She smells fried. Everything in the place smells just like her."

She comes over and hugs me.

I say, "Happy birthday," and in a few minutes I've put on a dress, and we're all running down the stairs to get in the jeep.

We head up Prospect Avenue to the Heights with Reuben's music on the tape deck and the whole car smelling like food and flowers.

I look at the sky and hope the storm holds off.

7

I CAN FOLLOW the shoes and clothes down the hall from our bedroom out to the living room. And from there I keep going ... down the four flights of stairs to the street. I figure I could have gone farther, but I see one of the street people wearing my sweatshirt.

She watches me pick up socks and bras, pants and shirts. She leans against the iron fence in front of our apartment building and starts pulling the sweatshirt over her head. I take two steps towards her and hand her a couple more shirts, then walk back up the stairs.

It started raining last night. Soft spring rain. I remember that I turned to the window to watch it mist over the streetlights and heard voices calling and people laughing below. You can hear everything outside when the weather starts warming up.

Funny how I could hear the street noises and the rain and not hear my own sister falling back. Falling back to sickness.

Aunt Shirley is wide awake when I come in. She sips on coffee, scattered clothes at her feet.

I flop on to the couch and start folding everything I have in my hands.

Aunt Shirley shakes her head, laughing. "Where in the world did you learn that you're supposed to fold underwear?"

I say, "Nowhere."

Aunt Shirley's nightgown has cows all over it. Even the bandanna around her head has cows on it. She says she's thinking about moving away from fish now, even though her ankle tattoo is of a rainbow trout. They are noble fish, she says; she won't eat 'em.

"While you were picking up the clothes, I called Reuben."

I nod my head, and all I can think is I'm glad that it's spring. I'm glad that it's warm. I'm glad that it's morning and not night and that Nikki won't freeze to death in the next twenty-four hours.

Aunt Shirley moves over and takes me in her arms. I'd like to stay this way for the rest of the day.

I can't deal with school. But I know if I mention it, Aunt Shirley will say I should go, and I won't feel good about fighting about it. So for the time being I stay wrapped in her arms with Nikki's damp clothes all around us.

23-year-old African-American female,
5'7", braids.

We still have posters from two years ago, when Nicole disappeared for three months. I sit on our bedroom floor and scratch out the 23 and put in 25. Twenty-five years and one day old. Gone again.

I look at the poster. Nicole's face hasn't changed. The medicine hasn't bloated her or broken out her skin.

One time she said she dared nature to do any more to her than it already had done.

25-year-old African-American female,
5'7", braids.

YOU HAVE TO WAIT twenty-four hours in this country before you can get the law involved when an adult is missing from home. I watch the news channel, eating sweet cereal out of the box. I sit and watch it for twenty-four hours.

A country changed governments in that time.

Scientists found fossils in a streambed in Iowa and a fish that they thought had been dead a million years in an ocean half-way around the world. A million years. Something was just living life for a million years without anyone giving it a thought.

And all this happened in twenty-four hours during a soft spring rain.

Part Two

8

WE NEVER HAVE TAKEN a newspaper. Never. If we have to, we watch television news, but Aunt Shirley says it's garbage; they tell you about things you can't do anything to help. So we didn't get to see the article on Nicole.

I had gone to school like I'd been doing for almost a week. I only half listened in English and stood in the middle of the room like a zombie during dance movement. I'd been going to the airport, looking for Nikki twice a day, never finding her.

The newspaper said that a young woman had wandered on to the airport runway. Airport officials couldn't say how it happened. I thought, She could have stayed hidden longer if the blackberries had been out on the bushes, but I'd still missed her.

After six and a half days, my sister sat in a police station in a pink nightgown and no shoes. The officer who brought her in said she had a beautiful singing voice but seemed a bit confused.

A reporter followed the police from the airport and was trying to talk to Nicole when Aunt Shirley walked into the station.

We'll never take a paper.

REUBEN PACES up and down the hall in brown hiking boots today, waiting for the doctor to come talk to us. Reuben was visiting one of his buddies in Arkansas the last time Nikki disappeared.

He quits walking and sits down next to Aunt Shirley.

"I should have seen it. She was squirming at her birthday party."

Aunt Shirley closes her eyes and leans back in a chair. They've remodelled the waiting room since we were last here. There's music playing over the sound system, a whole orchestra of bells. I want to get up and dance.

"She stopped taking the pills, Reuben. We can only do so much. She's a grown person. She's brilliant, and if she didn't want us to know, it wouldn't be a problem for her to fool us."

I feel like dancing to the bells 'cause I don't

want to hear what they're saying. I've heard it all before.

Reuben gets up and starts pacing again. "We still should have known. I mean, I know she could have gotten sick again even sticking with the pills."

Aunt Shirley opens her eyes. "It's always going to be this way, Reuben."

She says it real gently, but Reuben looks like he's been shot – like in the army. Shot a second time. Seems like he'll always be hurt bad by someone he knows. His buddy had accidentally shot him in the stomach in a training exercise, and now he's hit again, right in City Hospital.

I like City . . . It's got big windows in all the waiting rooms. There's no hospital smell. Must have taken 'em years to get rid of it 'cause the building's old.

I used to walk up and down the halls, looking into people's rooms. Sometimes I'd stand and watch them sleep. If they had the television on, I might stand there long enough for them to invite me in.

I've shared a lot of hospital meals and TV shows with strangers. I know there are rules; I'm supposed to be in a waiting room. But the nurses pretty much leave me alone.

Nicole likes City, too. Well, she always ends up here. Maybe she doesn't like it the way I do, but I don't think she minds it as much as some of the patients in the psychiatric ward.

She calls that the dropout ward. She laughs about it when she's well. She talks about the people she sees on a regular basis. Says she figures some of them are on the same breakdown clocks.

Aunt Shirley doesn't like to hear her talk like that.

Nicole says that it's okay, 'cause she has to laugh. She has to think that everything that might be funny *is* funny. She says she has to laugh hard to keep the whispers away.

NICOLE HAS SENT me a list of things to do from City:

Wash all her bedclothes

Find the bald-headed doll she used to play with

Wrap her tennis shoes in newspaper and put them under her bed.

Put the bald-headed doll in her window

Find all the pennies in the apartment and put them in jars

Make sure the radio volume dials are set to eight

Make sure that if I eat at Doggy's, I don't use the phone

Cover her fish chair with her blue sweater

Call the secondhand store on the corner and ask if they have blue sweaters

Take all her blue clothes and put them in a bag, then hide them in our closet

After Aunt Shirley hands me the list, she goes into her room and closes the door.

A long time ago I heard her telling one of her friends that Nicole's being sick was something I'd just have to live with. She said none of us would get out of this one untouched. Aunt Shirley's not sentimental. So I expect it when she gives me the list without a word.

I figure I'll do some of the things on it. I don't know where the bald-headed doll is. The big problem, though, is going to be putting the shoes under Nikki's bed, 'cause we never have taken a newspaper. Never.

9

MISS ONYX PHELPS is a dancer, too. She says that a dancer is always a dancer, even when the bones don't let you go on.

"But the best thing is chocolate," she tells me. "When I knew I was not going to dance any more, all I wanted to do was eat chocolate." Miss Onyx walks a little ahead of me as we cross to the park. She can move like most of the kids I know – and she's over eighty.

I pull up grass and let the wind scatter it from my hands.

"Did you go on diets?"

Miss Onyx laughs. "My dear little girl, I was always on a diet. You'll never know – you being so little."

She waves her hands in the air and shakes her head.

I love her accent. She says that she was born in Austria before Europe became sad. She finds a seat and pulls me down with her, holding my hands.

"All I wanted to do was dance. That was all. I was very beautiful. I know, I know we are not supposed to say these things about ourselves, but I was."

"Where did you dance?"

"Oh, I danced with a wonderful company in Vienna. I was very happy. I danced. I worked at my family's bakery – but mostly I loved life. So much was happening . . ."

Miss Onyx rubs my hands; hers are cold. Then she turns to watch some boys playing soccer on the field.

She'd told us all about Austria one afternoon when Nikki and I went to visit. She showed us many books about her country. They were all she had left, and that was only because her family had sent some of their things to America with neighbours who were escaping the Nazis. They expected to follow.

She cried over her family the day she told us.

She laughs now at the boys on the soccer field.

Miss Onyx turns around to face me. "Do you remember your parents enough to miss them, Sophy?"

I think about the one memory I have of them.

Flying. They must have flown me around a room in their arms together.

"I remember flying. That's all. I remember that I laughed and they laughed, too. I don't remember enough to miss them, though."

Miss Onyx settles back against the park bench.

"You know, the name I have now is only my stage name. My father would think it funny. He always called me his jewel. I thought of the name with him in mind."

I say, "I'm keeping Sophy. I think Sophy is a good name for a dancer . . . Do you think so?"

"I think Sophy is a fine name."

I'm keeping it for sure now. I flex my feet in my tennis shoes.

We walk back up the avenue. Miss Onyx talks about everything under the sun, and makes me laugh. When a couple of girls walk by in real big pants with shirts to their knees, she smiles. She stops in the middle of the sidewalk to watch them.

"Why are their clothes so big?"

I say, "It's just the style. Street – you know?"

She laughs. "What is 'street'?"

"What people wear in the street, I guess."

She likes the style and keeps on laughing until we get back to her apartment and she's offered me tea and chocolate. I accept both and wander around her living room.

A dancer's room. There's a glass cabinet with old ballet shoes and programmes in languages I can't read. Beside her big overstuffed flowered couch sits a basket of dried roses. I sit cross-legged in front of them. They are all the roses she had gotten for her first performance.

Miss Onyx sits on the couch and smiles.

"Very soon you will have baskets and baskets of roses. It will happen, Sophy, before you know. Nothing will happen to take it away from you. The war took my career from me. It just came ... and took many things away from people."

I don't know about any war. At least not like Miss Onyx. Reuben was in one a couple of years ago and doesn't talk about it. I think his music talks about it.

Miss Onyx is still talking about her life. She looks over at me suddenly.

"Sophy, have you ever thought about not dancing?"

"No, I never have."

"Can you imagine dancing being taken away from you, having no control any more of something that was given to you at birth?"

I shake my head. Miss Onyx rises, crosses to her lace-covered window, and looks out.

"Imagine your sister then. Imagine the loss she feels when she cannot come out of herself."

I start to cry because I think of Nicole the secret dancer, and all of it out of her control.

Miss Onyx comes back to the couch again. "That is why it's so important to use your gift. The more you use it, the more you will find yourself."

I didn't know I was lost and say so. Miss Onyx smiles and nods.

"Maybe you don't know you're not quite who you will be. There's more to come. Oh, yes. With you, I see more to come. Now drink the rest of your tea, and I will tell you about the time I danced for an empress."

Miss Onyx tells me stories that are magical, and she was in them.

When I get ready to leave, Miss Onyx takes a silver bracelet off her wrist. It has stones in it I've never seen. She puts the bracelet on my wrist and holds my hands real tight, then waves me away. The numbers on her wrist show now.

She whispers to me as she closes the door, "For a dancer."

10

"I 'M NOT READY YET," I tell them. But it was still my idea to come to the tower.

Paco and Jay Jr press against the big observation window with their backs to me, looking out over the city. Their whole bodies lean against the glass, and with their dark clothes on, they look like shadowy Xs against the sky – at least what you can see of it.

The terminal-tower window is covered with spiders. Huge ones. They've been here ever since I can remember. You'd think they'd have done something about 'em by now. They're my excuse, though, the reason I'm sitting here on the floor. I hope they stay on the window for ever so I'll never have to get that close to the edge. Must feel like you're dying, being that near to the clouds and not even flying in a plane.

I start counting the minutes before Paco and Jay are gonna get bored and leave the window. Too close to the clouds.

You have to change elevators to get to the top of the tower. The building is full of offices, and we rode up most of the way with people in suits. Wrong time of the day, too, 'cause we're supposed to be on a school field trip down the street at the Arcade. We sneaked past the teacher.

Paco turns around finally and says to me, "I think I can see Toledo."

Jay shakes his head. "No, you can't."

I know what they're doing, and it won't work. They want me to come settle the fight by looking out the window at something that's going to be one of the west suburbs; but little do they know I'll be dead before they can get any satisfaction out of my doing that. They always try this when we come up to the tower – but each time I keep comin' and not getting any closer.

I stay where I am on the floor. "I don't think you can see Toledo from here, and anyway those spiders are liable to come right through a crack in the window and poison us. We'd all probably be dead for a while before anybody found our bodies ..."

Jay and Paco start laughing and keep lookin' off into the spider-covered clouds.

I always wanted a tree house, and being up here

must take care of that feeling I have for one. From our apartment nobody looks like blots of colour. It's safe there, only four flights up, in our living-room window.

But I decided I had to get over my fear of going over to the window 'cause the other morning something happened. I woke up and my face had changed overnight. Just changed.

It wasn't anything I could put my finger on. I don't know if my mouth had changed or what. It just wasn't the me of the day before, or the day before that.

For a minute I thought maybe everything else had changed about me. Maybe I couldn't dance any more or even know any of the things that I've always known. So I decided to do something that I'd never done before.

Paco and Jay Jr are still looking out all over the city, and I'm still me, sitting cross-legged on the floor.

And I can't move.

I WALK REAL SLOW down the hall – looking at how Nicole has changed, wondering if she ever woke up different but not knowing how.

When I turn around to go back to the first drawing, Reuben is leaning against the wall, smiling.

"Do you think she's changed?"

I look all the drawings over again, slowly. "Yeah, in every picture she's a different person. How come, Reuben? People don't change that much, all the time."

He shrugs and walks into the living room. I notice after a visit with Nicole he's quiet. He lets me talk and talk if I want to, but he never seems to say much.

He does tell me everything that went on when he saw Nicole. They just held hands, he says. She isn't talking yet.

I THINK ABOUT the drawings as I walk home across the avenue. In one of them Nicole is almost bald. I remember the morning I swept all of her hair up off the bathroom floor.

Looking at her through the bathroom doorway, I watched how she examined her face in the mirror.

The memory is so fresh 'cause I'd had the same look myself just the other morning. Even though I'm on a street full of people and the buses are blowing by, I feel like I'm walking up narrow castle steps to a locked room.

When I walk by a record store and want to dance to the music coming out the door, I know I'm still outside the locked room. The feeling stays with me, though, until I hear Aunt Shirley in the kitchen.

The apartment smells like flowers and something

baking. I don't know exactly what it is. It smells like home. It feels like home. And when Aunt Shirley comes out of the kitchen with her head still wrapped up in a scarf from tofu, I know – it's home.

11

PROP YOUR FEET UP on the bench across from you at Doggy's and don't order anything the first or second time the waitress asks you what you want. You'll only do it once.

The first time I did it Doggy himself screamed from the kitchen, "What the hell do you want?" I slid under the table. The waitress stood there shaking her head, and I made up my mind quick.

I don't think there'll ever be a second chance.

I order three doughnuts and some mint hot chocolate, but I change the chocolate to orange juice when the waitress stares at me like I just told her to serve me two puppies on a plate.

No mint hot chocolate at Doggy's.

I got some pamphlets from a nurse at City

Hospital about schizophrenia. She gave me a brownie with the pamphlets.

Nicole is checking out of City. I've got all her favourite clothes packed, three outfits she can choose to come home in. I probably shouldn't pack that many. She's stable now. You gotta be stable to walk out of the hospital, but it still might be too many choices for her.

Got to make it easy for her to stay out of City this time.

I tried on all of Nicole's clothes this morning. Just took them all off their hangers and laid them across our beds. Aunt Shirley is working weekends so I have the whole place to myself. Me and the fish on the ceiling.

My sister doesn't go to malls. She buys most of her clothes at secondhand stores, but there's not as many of them as there used to be around here. Nicole's clothes are all beautiful. She'll shop for hours, picking and choosing. She's always there when they get new shipments in.

Nicole thinks it's a waste to buy new clothes. She figures if you wait long enough, everything will come back in style. I guess she's right.

I make like I hate going with her to the second-hand stores, but I've been looking in the windows of the stores the last few days. So many different people rummaging through the used things.

I saw this woman crawling underneath a rack of shirts. She probably hid a shirt until she could make up her mind about it. Nicole says that kind of stuff isn't fair. She says it'll give you bad karma. She's never done it, and she always gets the best picks.

I look over the pamphlets for a while, until all my doughnuts are gone, and signal to the waitress. She's telling somebody at the counter he's had enough caffeine. The man nods his head and orders milk.

I order a couple more doughnuts, and when I take a bite out of the first one, I see Jay Jr standing across the avenue, waiting for a bus. I run out and wave him over.

He looks kind of out of place with no Paco beside him.

I take his arm and motion for him to come with me into Doggy's to wait for the bus. You can see the bus a block away through big plate-glass windows.

Jay sits and reaches across for a doughnut.

I say, "What's up?"

He talks through a mouth of powdered-sugar doughnut.

"Headin' to the Heights. They got that comic-book store I always go to."

"I thought that place burned down."

"It did, but they moved across the street."

"Where could they move to? What's empty across the street?"

58

Jay takes a gulp out of my orange juice and points towards the window, then grabs my hand.

"Come on, you're not doing anything but sittin' here. Come, go with me."

I stuff the pamphlets in my backpack, toss too much money on the table for my food, and run across the street with him to catch the bus.

JAY JR TALKS about getting a job cleaning up after horses this summer. His eyes shine. The bus moves on through the city.

"Where's this?" I say.

"Twinsburg. My dad's got this friend who's got this friend . . ."

I lick the rest of the sugar from my fingers and elbow the man who's fallen asleep next to me, then on me. He wakes up, notices where he is, and pulls the cord. The bus driver ignores him and drives on. The man shrugs and goes back to sleep.

Jay twists his baseball cap around. "You working this summer?"

"No."

"Why not? You can get a job. Your aunt just has to sign those papers 'cause you're under sixteen."

"I don't think my aunt wants me to work. Anyway, I have to watch my sister."

"Watch your sister do what? I thought she was older than you."

I look out the window. Things are starting to get greener as the bus moves into the suburbs.

"Yeah, she's older than me. She's sick, though."

Jay Jr stretches his legs into the aisle. He's about six foot four and never has any room for his legs. I start wondering if I've ever told him about Nicole. I know he doesn't hang much with anyone but Paco, and I don't know if I've ever told Paco about Nicole. They're my best friends and they're probably the only people in school who don't know about my sister.

I should talk more.

The bus passes mansions and lots of brownstone apartments. Trees, trees, trees. I could live here. If Aunt Shirley ever makes it and tofu is a thing of the past, I want to live by the trees.

The bus drops us off in the business section. I see the man tumble over as the bus pulls off.

I GOT THESE gigantic chocolate cookies for Miss Onyx at the bakery next to the comic-book store. They're chocolate, chocolate. They're so warm they almost melt in the bag. I walk up the avenue towards her building. Reuben's jeep is in front, with him on top of it.

Miss Onyx sits on the stoop, laughing at something that Reuben has said. The sun reflects off her bright red hair.

I raise the cookies above my head. "I come bringing chocolate."

Miss Onyx claps her hands, and Reuben shakes his head and smiles. "You been hopping all over the city, Sophy?"

I hand the bag of cookies to Miss Onyx, taking one out for Reuben, and say, "Not the city but the Heights. I went with a friend to a comic-book store."

Once I've climbed on top of the jeep beside Reuben, Miss Onyx says, "They have stores with nothing but comic books now?"

"Yeah, they do," Reuben tells her.

Miss Onyx chews on the cookies and watches some kids across the street skateboarding over a fire hydrant. She looks like she's watching magic as the sun starts to go down over the city.

I take the pamphlets out of my backpack and think about Nicole coming home. I spread the pamphlets in front of me like cards. Reuben picks one of the brochures, opens it, begins to read, then drops it and puts his arm around me.

"I know you're going to be happy to get your sister back."

I watch Miss Onyx watching me from the stoop, and my hand goes to the silver bracelet.

I say, "The house won't be so quiet any more."

12

THEY GOT A WHOLE AISLE of sunglasses in the drugstore across from the empty lot that I used to play in. All kinds of sunglasses. I slip two pairs in my pocket and am walking on Euclid Avenue before I know it. Cool and calm. Cool and calm.

THIS MORNING'S LIST:

Wash last night's dishes
Buy paper plates
Remind Nicole to take medicine when she gets home
Pick up toothpaste at drugstore (try again today)
Remember the things on the list

I remember everything on the list.

I walk past the bus station and decide to go in to get a pop from the one machine that won't just take your money. I like the bus station and come here when I can – at least once a week these days. Aunt Shirley says all bus stations remind her of giant toilets. I like them, though.

There was this woman once who was going to meet a man she hadn't seen in forty-five years. She'd sat on one of the chairs surrounded by baskets held together with twine and boxes marked FRAGILE. I'd sat next to her and offered her some of my potato chips. Her hair was twisted on top of her head with a barrette of rhinestones. I got her a pop 'cause she said she'd been sitting for a couple of hours and couldn't leave her things. Her bus wasn't scheduled for a while.

She told me she'd loved the man she was going to see for fifty years, but they had married other people. When one of them was free, through divorce or death, the other was married. They'd written to each other all that time. They were both seventy, and she was going to Michigan to live with him.

There's always something going on at the bus station. Always something.

Aunt Shirley puts her hands on her hips and shakes her head when I tell her bus-station stories. She laughs at some of them and usually feels the same way I do about the people in them.

To stay in the bus station, though, you have to

pick an adult to sit next to or security will throw you out for loitering. More than once I've almost been thrown out when there weren't any interesting adults to sit next to. It's a challenge.

I walk to the pop machine and take my time picking what I want and look around. For a Saturday it's pretty quiet. A whole bunch of buses must have just left. I decide to get my pop and go, but then I see the man out of the corner of my eye.

He's standing near the water fountain, talking to someone who's not there. His hands move, and he nods and shakes his head. His whole body moves to a rhythm nobody but him will ever hear. I can't move. I stand staring; then my head starts to move like his.

The spell is broken when a security guard goes over to him and starts talking. It is a spell. I am right there – with him in his head. I run out of the bus station and put on my sunglasses. Cool and calm.

WE'RE FORTY-FIVE MINUTES late picking Nicole up from City. Reuben's managed to hit every street that's under construction in Cleveland. He hums and looks cool, though.

Aunt Shirley's hands tense around the bottle of pop she's been drinking.

Nicole is sitting cross-legged in front of the hospital when we pull up to the kerb. She's talking to a woman I've seen before. The woman sits next to her on the only strip of grass City has. She nods her head to everything Nicole says.

My sister is all in blue. She looks up and smiles at us for a second when I shout from the jeep. She blows us kisses and keeps on talking. The woman keeps nodding.

And I remember a song Nicole sometimes sings: *All dressed in blue, who are you?*

"I'M NOT HERE."

I put my book down and look at Nicole.

I ask, "What did you say?"

Nicole swings her feet to the back of the couch and lets her head hang over the seat cushions. She's wearing men's pyjamas that she bought from the secondhand store the day she got home from City. She'd stayed in the store almost five hours, touching and feeling clothes that used to belong to other people.

Aunt Shirley told me, "Just let her be."

The only thing Nikki came out with were the pyjamas. They were white silk. I bet the rich man who owned them would be surprised about where they ended up. Probably has so many pairs he doesn't even know they're gone.

"I said, I'm not here. The medicine makes me feel like I'm not here. Any minute what's left of me could float away."

"Must be strange," I say.

Nicole smiles and stretches, upside-down. "What's strange, Sophy? I really don't know any more."

I almost tell her about waking up changed a few weeks ago and about the man at the bus station, but don't. It's too scary to think about. She was my age when she walked out of the store into the parking lot ...

I listen to the street sounds below us, to the traffic, then I hear the saxophone.

Reuben is standing below the window, playing. Nicole and me sit in the big window and listen. I wish I knew music. All I know is what I can dance to. I grab Nicole's hand and pull her out to the middle of the floor.

We swing each other around the painted fish chair until the room is nothing but a blur of colour. When we fall to the rug after a few minutes, Reuben is still playing in the courtyard, leaning against the iron fence.

We sit in the window again and a breeze blows across us and ruffles Nicole's silk pyjamas.

She wraps her arms around me and whispers, "It's like a concert, isn't it?"

I nod and touch the sunglasses in my shirt pocket.

13

A LIST OF THINGS I'VE ... FOUND:

2 pairs of sunglasses
4 silver rings
32 candy bars
4 lipsticks
10 CDs (no CD player)
5 books
A wrench
2 pints of paint
4 dish towels
A flower bouquet
2 cans of lima beans

I keep everything in a box under the bed. I wear

the things I can, when I can. Sometimes it's hard. Aunt Shirley stared at the silver rings for a long time the other night at dinner. They match my bracelet so nice ... The salesgirl loved them. So do I.

The rings are old. Estate jewellery, the girl said. I don't know what that means, but probably some person who isn't living any more used to wear them.

I found Nicole sitting by my bed an hour ago, looking in the box. When she heard me come in the room, she glanced up for a second, then went back to all the things piled in there.

She said, "What's this stuff?"

She was holding up the two cans of lima beans. She started reading the ingredients. She turned them around and shook them, like maybe they were joke cans of beans. I guess she thought something would spring out.

I walked over real chilled. I took the beans out of her hands and put them back in the box.

"It's a school thing. We're supposed to get stuff together and make our own time capsule."

It was a bad lie. And it was the first time I ever told one to Nicole. I waited for something to happen to me. The floor should open up or all the cats in the neighbourhood, their hair should fall out. Doggy's would probably disappear in a sinkhole. Something bad would happen, what with me lying to my sister.

The lying had been too easy. People lied all the time, but I thought it would be harder.

The really hard part was what I was thinking when Nicole smiled, then got up and left. Lying to my poor sick sister. It was a hurtin' thought. I'd heard people call her that before: "Your poor sick sister."

I unwrapped a candy bar, broke it in four parts, then threw them in the wastepaper can in the hall.

WHEN I WAS LITTLE, every prize I ever got out of a box of Cracker Jack was a book. That would be okay now, but when you're five and can barely read ... I always wanted a magnifying glass or a spinning top but never got one. Nicole would always trade with me, 'cause she was kinda old for the prizes anyway. It wasn't the same, though.

I wonder if she remembers always having to give me her prize. I feel like I was never able to give Nicole anything of value. Never. I don't think any of us ever can.

We can care about her – love her – but what else? She's too old for Cracker Jack prizes, and it'll never be like it was when I couldn't read.

14

THE PEOPLE NEXT DOOR have finally moved in. They've got a dance *barre* in their attic – and nothing else. Just like in the movies. Nicole saw it first. She was on her hourly look-out. Lookin' out the window.

She goes from room to room, looking for Them, I think. Staring out Aunt Shirley's room, she found the *barre*. Nicole says I should knock on their door, introduce myself, and ask if they'd let me dance in their attic.

She would.

She's always doing that kind of stuff. It never used to bother me, but lately . . .

I sit on Aunt Shirley's bed now and look into the round attic windows across the way. It looks like an attic should look, I guess; I've never been in one.

Wood floors and slanted walls. The ceiling is high, though. I could dance in that room.

I pull my new hooded sweatshirt over my head and toss it on Aunt Shirley's floor. It has CLEVELAND STATE printed up the arms. I can only wear it around home; wouldn't want the person missing it to start wondering.

I could really dance for ever in that attic room.

MISS ONYX POINTS at a photo on the wall. "She danced until she couldn't any more."

The woman she's talking about is framed in black and white – surrounded by flowers. It's an old picture, like all the other ones.

Nicole gets up from beside Miss Onyx and touches all the pictures on the walls. She walks softly. On her toes.

She's been going in and out. Some days are better for her. Today is a good one, so she came out of the apartment with me to visit Reuben. Most of the way she almost skipped down the avenue.

Reuben wasn't home when we got to his apartment, so Nicole is with me, wandering all over Miss Onyx's living room. She touches the lace on the curtains and looks on the bookshelves.

Miss Onyx watches her. Smiling.

"See anything interesting? I keep everything."

Nicole sits on the floor, taking some books with her.

"You have some old things."

Miss Onyx nods her head.

Nicole flips through one book and sits it beside her. "You're old, I guess, so your things go with you."

Miss Onyx laughs until there are tears coming out of her eyes. Nicole looks at her like she doesn't know what's so funny. I wonder if she's taking her medicine.

Nicole and Miss Onyx talk about everything and nothing for the next hour, with Miss Onyx laughing at the things Nicole says and finally Nicole just laughing, because.

And I think, My sister laughed like this that warm day at the cemetery. That day it almost rained, but didn't.

I'D WORN A DRESS to Nicole's party. It was gauze and looked good spread out over the grass. It swung around and caught every bit of breeze that blew by us.

I'd walked over to all the headstones I knew so well and said a quiet hello. I'd been coming to the cemetery so long, I knew all the names of everyone around Mama and Daddy. They were like neighbours who you only saw a couple times a year. You'd say hello and go back to your business.

On the grass near Mama and Daddy, Aunt Shirley and Reuben had spread the quilt from the back of our couch.

I can't really remember seeing the man with the bagpipes walking towards us. I only remember his being there.

He'd sat down on a headstone about twenty yards away. He'd adjusted his pipes and straightened the cap on his head. Then he'd played.

I'd never been so close to such sounds. The pipes cried. They just cried right there. Aunt Shirley leaned over and whispered in Nicole's ear. Nicole sat and listened, in another world, while Reuben stretched out on the reds and greens of the quilt and closed his eyes.

The bagpipe man kept on playing. The longer he played to his relative, the darker the sky became. I thought the rain wouldn't hold back much longer, but it did.

After a few songs we realized we'd have music most of the afternoon, so we settled down to it. The pipes were like warm water rushing over me.

We ate good that day. Ribs from the market and flowers everywhere. Nicole covered her legs with daisies and ate until she looked dazed. I'd got the same look sooner. I had to eat to stay awake. After a while the music, food, and flowers were too much for me. I went to sleep to soft voices and music from someplace I'd never been.

I woke up alone. The man with the pipes was gone, too. I felt for warmth on the quilt and found none. I remember crawling over flowers and mugs and reading BELOVED BROTHER AND PARENT. Mama, Daddy, and me, together. I went back to sleep, not worried about anything.

Aunt Shirley woke me with a warm hand on my head. It took a long time to wake up. When I did, I noticed Reuben and Nicole were nowhere in sight.

Aunt Shirley said, "She's gone," and that's all.

We put the plates and cups back in the picnic basket. Then wrapped the leftovers and folded the quilt.

Aunt Shirley took all the flowers but one and spread them around my parents' graves. We sat against the stones and waited for Reuben to come back. I leaned against Aunt Shirley and slept again.

I've been sleeping through bad things for a long time. I miss everything bad that happens. I even get sleepy when I get into arguments with people. The school psychologist calls it a sleep reflex and told Aunt Shirley not to worry about it.

She worries, though. She's scared for me.

I don't remember walking back to Reuben's jeep or walking up the four flights of stairs to our apartment. I do remember Paul and Earl opening my bedroom door and whispering that I looked fine to them. I heard them moving around the living room and wondered where Aunt Shirley might be.

She'd left the daisy in a jelly glass on my night table. The daisy stood tall, lookin' out the window.

It wasn't there in the morning, though. I slept through my sister coming home and leaving again in her nightgown. I slept through her pulling out everything in our drawers and lining all her blue clothes up against the wall.

NICOLE IS STILL laughing at something Miss Onyx has said. I'm back in the living room with its pictures of dancers and its books.

Nicole comes over and puts a dried flower in my hair.

She whispers, "You'll have more than enough flowers in your arms one day. They'll throw them after you dance, Sophy."

Miss Onyx smiles from across the room.

I take the flower out of my hair. It's a rose. When we get home, I put it on my night table in a jelly glass, then go into Aunt Shirley's room and look into the attic next door.

15

LUMP WILLOW DOESN'T sound like a dancer's name. It is. Lump Willow doesn't look like a lump either, but he says he used to. This is the first year I've had Lump for modern dance.

He dances with a fedora on his head and wears an old football jersey. I stay after school to watch him work out. He dances on air. I want to float the way he does; I want to move like I don't have bones in my body. Like him.

I've decided he's the best and tell him so when he stops to drink coffee from a thermos.

He says, "Thanks. Haven't seen you around for a while."

"Been going home after school ... Things to do."

Lump Willow is the tallest dancer I've ever seen.

When he walks down the hall in school, you can see his head during a class change even if you're standing at the end farthest from him.

He sits down on the floor, and it squeaks under his weight. The sun shines off his head. He keeps it shaved and laughs when you mention it. The fedora's fallen off.

Lump points and flexes his feet while he sits in a straddle.

"What kinds of things have you been doing, miss? I thought you told me you needed the extra dance time."

"I do."

"Then what's up?"

Ever know somebody who looks right through you, somebody who knows when you're about to lie?

I say, "I got this kind of job after school. It takes up most of my time."

Before I can grab my backpack and leave, Lump is up and doing an arabesque. He doesn't dance to any music. The dust starts to fly. I don't know why, but all I want to do is cry. I watch him twirl, stop, and start again before he takes a breath and calls to me from across the room.

"Too bad about your job."

I think of catching the bus and going to the mall. Hanging out is my job lately. Finding things and hanging out. That's my job for now.

I ask, "Why too bad?"

"It's too bad because I have this friend who's going to need some help this summer. She has a dance studio. You know – little kids who dance like elephants – tap, ballet, et cetera. Thought you might like that kind of thing."

I do, but say no, wave, and run out the door to the stairs. I'm on a bus going down the avenue to the mall, thinking about why people say no when they really mean yes.

YOU CAN WALK, stay in each store for ten minutes, and still not make it through half of the mall in a day. Mostly I sit and watch everybody. I sit at the boring end of the mall. It's happening over by the food court. All the good stores are there, and they watch you ...

I open my backpack and take out a candy bar. From the box under my bed. Didn't want anything at lunch. I'd sneaked into a practice room with Jay Jr and listened to him play piano.

Jay plays piano and paints, and his dad doesn't want him doing any of it. Wants Jay to be an engineer. Jay says his dad wants him to live in Shaker Heights and ride the rapid to an office with white walls and a secretary named Sloan.

His dad works at the Ford plant.

All Jay wants to do is move to the Flats and paint.

78

Aunt Shirley wants me to do anything that's going to keep me out of jail. Until a while ago I was doing just that.

I throw the candy bar in the can next to me by the bench. I haven't been able to eat one yet.

I love the towel store, the colours and fabrics and the way the corner with all the soaps smells. The aisles go on for ever with towels, rugs, and bath mats piled ten feet over your head.

I've been thinking of getting some nice beach towels for the airport. Nicole never worries about sitting in the dirt, but I do.

I find some nice ones with seashells on them, white towels with shells in pink and green. I daydream of Nicole and me lying on them, watching the planes, taking a thermos of tea.

Then something happens.

Nicole turns to me and looks exactly like I did the morning I woke up, looked in the mirror, and had changed . . .

The towels feel like sandpaper as I stuff them into my backpack and leave the store.

All through the mall I watch my face in the store windows. I'm looking for another change, I guess. I'm looking for another me. I started finding things after the first change.

I stop and watch the big-screen television in the video store until I'm sure I'm going to be okay.

I lean against the bench at the bus stop, not wanting to sit down 'cause I don't think I'll have enough energy to get up. I hope I get a seat near the door. It won't take much for me to just fall down the steps at the stop for Doggy's.

I PULL ONE of the beach towels out of my backpack and spread it across a booth at Doggy's. I ask the waitress what the special is. Fried fish.

"Is it fresh?" I say.

She puts her hands on her hips and shakes her head. "It's fresh if you think sitting a couple of months in a cardboard box with breading on it would qualify as fresh."

I lean back on the beach towel and close my eyes.

I say, "I'll take it."

Fried breaded fish and a seashell towel at Doggy's is the next best thing to the beach.

THE APARTMENT IS EMPTY. Aunt Shirley is working late at tofu, and there's no telling where Nicole has wandered off to. There's a message from Reuben to her that she should call him. I like his voice on tape. It's like cool water on a hot day.

I head for Aunt Shirley's room and take a beach towel out again. I look into the attic next door and wrap the towel around my waist. All I want to do is dance like Lump Willow and Miss Onyx, but I think it won't ever happen.

It won't ever happen 'cause I think I might be losing my mind. If I lose my mind, the only thing I'll ever be is a secret dancer with a stolen bouquet of flowers under my bed.

16

THE BEACH TOWEL is still wrapped around me. I don't remember leaving the apartment like this. I look around Miss Onyx's living room and know I can sleep here. It's getting where I can't sleep next to my own sister. Dreams and shadows. Too many dreams and shadows.

"You all right, child?"

Miss Onyx owns only cotton blankets. Soft cotton blankets. She says that in the concentration camp there was no softness. Her clothes scratched and there were no sheets. She says that the only softness there was in her memories: her parents, her old house, and the park that she used to play in as a child. There was softness in her memories of everything that had been her life until the world fell apart.

She says all she wanted was to be held in a blanket by her mother. That would make it all right.

Miss Onyx holding me in a blanket is just fine with me. Just fine. I drift towards sleep with classical music playing on the radio and the soft tinkling of a cup and saucer. Miss Onyx sips tea next to me on the couch. The living room smells of peppermint, lemon, and soft memories.

I curl up tighter in the blanket. "Yes, ma'am," I say. "Just fine."

I'D WALKED to Miss Onyx's apartment in a fine rain. I'd hoped for puddles.

When I walked out of our apartment and down the avenue and saw the dancing woman across the street, I decided that I wouldn't be coming back. The woman was in the rain, dancing in a slip, and a bunch of little kids were sitting on the balcony right above the sidewalk, laughing.

She stopped dancing and looked at me for a second. She smiled, then started splashing into the gutters.

AUNT SHIRLEY is sitting by me when I wake. I still smell peppermint. It's night now.

"Nice place to crash, huh?"

I rub my eyes and look at the dancers on the wall.

"Real nice. What time is it?"

Aunt Shirley looks at her watch and shakes her head.

"Ten."

I say, "Sorry," as she leans over me and brushes my forehead with her lips.

I look over at Miss Onyx in her big overstuffed chair. She keeps reading her book and doesn't look up or tell Aunt Shirley what I told her when I showed up this afternoon, crying.

"It's just a beach towel I got at the mall."

Aunt Shirley laughs. Her face is warm in the soft glow of the table lamp. I sink down farther in the cotton blanket.

When we get ready to leave, Miss Onyx says, "Keep this child beside you as long as you can," then gently pushes me to Aunt Shirley. We leave Miss Onyx and head down the avenue.

Aunt Shirley asks, "Are you okay? I called to you from the bus window. You just kept walking, not looking back. I thought . . ."

I put my head on her shoulder and nod, noticing for the first time the blanket wrapped around me.

Part Three

17

MAYBE IT WAS the birds singing, kicking the last of the snow off their feathers and hoping the winter is over. Not sure. I'm thinking, I learned to whistle in April, when I was six.

It's still too early in the day to go to school, but the woman next door is out front, digging in her yard. I guess she doesn't know this neighbourhood. Aunt Shirley said she talked to her, and the woman thinks there'll be flowers everywhere.

Aunt Shirley said the flowers'll grow from pure will. Evangaline Macon, our new neighbour, will make them grow by just standing over them, watching. Then she asked me if I thought Evangaline's name was powerful.

Yes.

I wave to Evangaline as I go out the gate and decide to be late for school by hanging at Doggy's for a while.

When I get to the end of the block and turn around, she's still watching me with her hands on her hips. I feel guilty and change my mind about Doggy's.

Aunt Shirley is right about her. It's like she sees. I don't know what it is. Maybe she sees that I want something that she has. I can't ask her about the *barre*.

I reach 36th just as Paco and Jay Jr get off the cross-town bus.

Paco hands me all his books and sits down in the middle of the sidewalk, while Jay runs across the street to call his grandmother. He's forgotten his books. Again.

"We got the tickets to the rap show. You going?" Paco holds out the tickets and lowers his cap over his eyes.

I nod and listen to my stomach growl. "Oh, yeah, I'm going."

Jay is done with his call and puts his arm around me as we go through the metal detector. Usually he stocks up on metal things just to drive the guards crazy. As we go through, he nods at the guard he usually gives a hard time.

He says, "I forgot my metal today."

We walk to our lockers on the second floor. I pass

Lump Willow's room just as he comes out his door. He smiles and takes his hat off.

It's a shame. I mean about me being so scared of losing my mind I can't even take him up on his offer of a summer job.

He bows.

Once i found Nicole's name carved in the moulding on the floor of one of the practice rooms in school. She'd carved mine there, too. It even had a date on it. Ten years ago. I was four. She knew I was coming.

Nicole used to walk around these halls and not eat in the cafeteria, just like me. She danced and played the piano.

When she'd come home, I'd follow her from room to room. I'd watch her unpack her dance clothes and shoes, then put them on – hopping around the room. I always wore a shirt dragging the ground and toe shoes falling off my feet. Nicole would sit cross-legged in the middle of the floor, smiling.

I can see our apartment from the hall window on the fifth floor of 36th Street School. I saw Nicole sitting on our roof once. A beach, right on top of the building, off the avenue.

I think I might be reliving Nicole's life. If she knew, Aunt Shirley would tell me, No, it isn't so.

But she watches me.

She's been watching since she picked me up that night at Miss Onyx's apartment. It's okay with me, just as long as she doesn't watch too hard.

After Aunt Shirley walked me home, I had a nightmare about planes. I'd had it before – that's why I go the airport with Nicole; she's making it her mission to help me get over being afraid.

But looking at her lying in bed, talking about blue clothes, scares me more . . .

I CHANGED in the mirror again. It could have been the light. It could have been the mirror. But I don't think it was either of them. My sister's been lying in bed for the last few days. She was in bed two mornings ago when I changed.

She hasn't been able to raise her head and says her medicine leaves her feeling like an elastic person. She says time is just stretching in front of her – pulling her along. She's hearing Them again. Whispers.

Last night I couldn't sleep in the room with Nikki. I lay on the couch until I heard the church bell two blocks away ringing 3.00 a.m. When I crawled under my quilt, the one on the couch, all I heard were the street women laughing down by the fence. No whispers.

After that, I listened for Aunt Shirley's breathing. I slowed my own down and blacked Nicole's out of my mind.

Aunt Shirley's breathing comforted me when I was little. Just her breathing. What could be easier?

I read in the dictionary:

schizophrenia: a mental disorder characterized by separation between thought and emotions, by delusions, bizarre behaviour, etc.

All these years I'd never looked the word up in the dictionary. I had pamphlets. Aunt Shirley had books. I'd listened to doctors as I leaned against Aunt Shirley in their leather offices. She always included me when she could. She said I should know everything.

One doctor didn't see it that way, but Aunt Shirley told him he would never be expected to have Nicole living with him. He let me stay.

Glad I finally checked the dictionary out. It didn't say anything about seeing changes in the mirror, but I had the feeling that might come under *delusions*.

Reuben's been coming over. He sits next to Nicole's bed for at least two hours a day. He talks to her even when she's asleep. When he's not talking, he's playing love songs to her on his saxophone.

He told me they're love songs.

He props his boots up on the nightstand and plays. Sometimes Nicole will toss in her sleep and sigh. Reuben says that the music is getting through despite all the drugs.

Once I heard Nicole ask Reuben why he wanted to be with her after all the years. Reuben told her that he just couldn't think of anyone else to love.

I should have known he'd be playing love songs for her.

Soft memories.

IN COMPOSITION we are supposed to write a one-hundred-word essay on the state of the world as we see it. I write:

Poverty in the cities
No housing for the homeless
War, hunger, pollution, war
Shootings
AIDS
Killing endangered species
People can't read
People don't care
People don't care
People don't care
People don't care
Mental illness
People don't care
Too many storms off the lake
Mental illness
Tornado season is close

I give Ms Tate two copies – which make a hundred words.

When I pass the big window on the fifth floor, I look across the rooftops and see Nicole again sitting on a lawn chair on our roof, near the smokestack.

I turn and whistle past the window like Reuben whistles past graveyards.

I look at the sky. A storm's coming.

18

NIGHT IN THE CITY. I sit at the foot of Nicole's bed and listen to her hoarse breathing. I want to wake her up and go for a walk.

A few years ago I used to worry about tornadoes getting her. She'd be so tired and sleepy on her medication that she wouldn't be able to run for the basement.

I check the sky again. Still worried, I guess.

I watch the women calling to one another on the street below and a few kids playing soccer. Everybody glows in the streetlights. I shake as a plane flies over, too low.

"WHAT'S WRONG, Sophy?"

I crawl from the foot of Nicole's bed to her pillow. She's sitting against the headboard, staring at me.

"Nothing's wrong now," I say.

She stretches, then rolls over on her side. "What was wrong before?"

"I thought it might storm –"

"And I'd sleep through it."

I snuggle up next to her and nod in the darkness. I know the light hurts her eyes after she's slept all day.

She says, "I thought we had this storm thing behind us. I mean, I thought you'd grown out of it."

"I guess I haven't."

Nicole finds my hand in the dark and squeezes it.

"It's up to me to help you get over it."

I say, "Why you?"

"Why not me?"

She lets go of my hand and gets up out of bed. She leans a little to the left and stands in the middle of the room for a while. She looks like one of my rag dolls, trying to walk.

She leaves the room, and a minute later I hear her crash against something in the living room. When I get there, she's taking pills from under the Buddha – lining them up on the coffee table.

She says, "I hope it storms before we go back to sleep, Sophy. They're not so bad, storms."

Nikki spins the Buddha on the table.

I go to the big window and look out. My reflection hasn't changed. I smile for a long time into the glass.

Nikki comes up behind me and wraps her arms around me.

She's waiting for the storm over the city. And she's waiting to tell me about all of it. I can feel it in her breathing.

I watch our reflections in the window. Nicole hugs me so tight that we look like one person. She shakes.

"That day we followed an old dog all over the city."

I stiffen up. "What day?"

Nicole acts like she hasn't heard me.

"He was a scraggy old dog. Bony. Looked like nobody ever loved him. We petted him awhile, then he ran off. I pulled you after him and me. We went all over the city.

"You wouldn't believe all the places there are to hide in the city. After a few days we started eating wherever the dog did. We slept where he slept –"

"How long?"

Nicole jumps. "Huh?"

"I said, how long were we following the dog, Nikki?"

"Days, weeks, I don't remember. It rained almost every day. We slept in a Dumpster once during a bad storm. I think you screamed through all the thunder. It echoed."

My face is wet now, but I don't know when I'd started crying.

"Did you think about taking me home? I mean, I was a little kid. I was scared, wasn't I?"

Nicole unwraps her arms from me and slides to the floor.

"Yeah, Sophy, but I thought we'd be safe in the Dumpster. I mean, it was one of those huge plastic ones. I had to tell you a scary story about a plane to get you in it ..."

"What story was that?"

I watch my sister draw designs only she sees on the floor. Her doctor has been talking about giving her injections that each last thirty days. She wouldn't have to count on herself for sanity any more. The Buddha could be just a piece of art.

Nicole says, "People used to care what happened to kids. There was only one person who even gave us food, I think ..."

A memory came to me.

I was sitting in Doggy's when I saw a girl around my age with a smaller girl. They stood leaning against the telephone pole outside. They stared at Doggy's window. They had big hungry eyes.

I bought a handful of doughnuts and two cokes, then walked out the door and handed everything to the girls. I got a warm flash when the older one nodded at me and took the food. When I turned at the door, they were gone.

They'd probably run around to the alley at the

back of the diner. I'd seen some kids hanging out there before.

Never had bought anybody food before, though. Aunt Shirley says growing up in the city hardens you to some things. I was so used to seeing kids living on the streets ...

I thought about those girls, though. There was something about them that made my stomach turn to water. I sat in Doggy's, waiting for them to come back. They didn't.

I look at Nicole's eyes. I turn to the window; the storm has really got going. I can't see my own eyes because of the flashes of light over the city, but I know my eyes look just like those of the two girls outside of Doggy's yesterday.

19

THE NUMBERS on Miss Onyx's wrist are blue, and she's going to have them the rest of her life. She says she's never thought of having them covered up. Scars.

Nicole came home once with an eight-inch scar on the back of her leg. Couldn't tell us how she got it. It was one of the first times I remember Aunt Shirley crying. She went in her room, closed the door, and cried like a baby. I leaned against her door for hours. More scars.

I DON'T SIT on the roof much these days. But I came up here because of Nicole. It's something. The city, the lake, and everything in between and around.

A few minutes ago I watched my sister stick her hand in boiling water. I just looked at her, not believing it was really happening. She smiled at me before her hand went under.

I guess my screaming brought Aunt Shirley running 'cause it sure wasn't Nikki's. She was still smiling after Aunt Shirley slathered burn ointment all over her hand and dragged her out the door to the hospital.

I walk over to the edge of the roof and close my eyes. This must be what it's like. This must be what it's like to lose all control. It must be like the great beyond. Farther than that even, but I know I've never felt even half as close to the edge.

It still scares me, though, so I decide to get off the roof and head for the street.

I WATCH MYSELF as a sales-clerk watches me steal beaded necklaces at Cool Joe Monkey. I look pretty good on the big television screen and forget that if I can see myself, so can almost everybody in the city . . .

At least everybody at Cool Joe's.

The beads are for the box under my bed. It's pretty full now, and sometimes, at night, I go through it.

At first, all the things would make me feel good. My things. I'd count them and put them on. But lately the box is filling too fast, and I don't know where I'll put everything.

I drop the necklaces in my T-shirt pocket and keep looking around.

Cool Joe's stuff I've never seen anywhere, and he keeps getting more of it in. The store smells like incense and fast food – Taco Heaven, across the street.

When the clerk puts his hand on my shoulder and asks me to come with him, I don't think about running. I go quietly.

Cool Joe Monkey is even stranger in the back.

I think I even saw a skeleton.

The clerk – maybe sixteen and in jeans and sandals – is about six foot seven. He holds out his hand to me and motions me to a chair.

"Mason," he says.

"Huh?"

"I said my name is Mason. Can you tell me how long you intend to keep stealing from us?"

I take the chair and think about the look on everybody's face when they hear about this. I'll only be able to go to Doggy's, where people like me hang out all day long drinkin' coffee and eatin' day-old doughnuts. Anywhere else, everybody would talk.

Mason and I stare at each other till it's clear I won't be saying a word.

He leans against the doorway and points me out.

He doesn't ask for the necklaces. I head past the door – putting on my sunglasses. Don't ever look back at the scene of a crime.

The look on Mason's face was so sad . . .

The necklaces burn through to my skin as I walk the avenue. I feel 'em. Scorching me. Even my tears are running hot down my face.

I WOULD PUT it all in a list, but I can't believe the amount of stuff I've found. It's too much. Anyway, the kids across the street love everything. I watch from the window. I have to put my bedroom light out. The kids' heads glow under the streetlights.

Some of the women pick out a few things.

I had to carry it all down in three smaller boxes. The canned food, I guess . . .

Nicole didn't pay attention to me as I dragged everything from under my bed. Her right hand was totally bandaged.

She talked to me while I packed everything, but her talk wasn't about what was in the box and where I was taking it. She talked about traffic.

Traffic signs, lights, jams . . .

I watched my sister's face. She was having a good time. She was still talking when I dragged the first box out of the room. By the time the last box went down, she was going on about road construction, and I thought I'd made a mistake, giving everything away. She's on heavy painkillers for her hand.

But then I remembered Mason's face from Cool Joe's.

I go down into the street and pick up the three boxes. They're empty now. I put them in the Dumpster on the side of the building, then sit on the stoop.

Aunt Shirley comes down the walk, carrying a bag, and heads towards the apartment building. She stops and talks to one of the street women for a second, laughs, and walks on.

"What you up to, sister?" Aunt Shirley asks when she sees me.

I say, "Not much."

She sets her bag down on the stoop.

"Not much, huh?"

She takes my hand, looks up towards our apartment, and shakes her head.

"There's always something, baby, always something."

20

T HE RAIN AND a night-
mare woke me. Nikki
was dancing in the dream. She was dancing over trash
cans and broken glass, during a thunderstorm. I was
crouched in a corner, and everything in the world was
bigger than me.

Nikki's dancing wasn't joyful. It was fast, frantic,
and scared me worse than anything ever has. I
realized when it was happening that the dream was
real. Had been real.

I know it now. It was the beginning . . .

I remember once telling Nikki I wanted to be just
like her. I was little and didn't know. Couldn't know.
She'd smiled at me.

*

I don't think anything could be as bad as this. Nicole's taken to mumbling to herself and answering her own questions. I watch her walk up and down the living room. Back and forth, past the furniture. She always stops to look out the window.

Her steps are evenly numbered every time.

Ten across the room and ten back.

She asks me if I know the time – twenty times in five minutes.

I run to the bathroom mirror – just to make sure. Nicole follows me, though. Her reflection shows in the mirror before mine.

There's nothing in the world worse…

ONCE NICOLE got a concussion when she was being taken to the hospital. She threw herself down the front stairs of the school. Lump Willow caught her before her whole body crashed into the cement. I stood beside Aunt Shirley, holding on to her shirt. They'd called her at tofu.

Nicole had broken down while practising after school. That's when I knew even dancing couldn't save her. Me and Aunt Shirley sure couldn't, but I was young, and I thought something as magical as dancing could.

I want to love Nicole like I used to. Nicole says

being schizophrenic is like screaming in a closet where no one can hear you . . .

She keeps pacing

SOPHY IS WATCHING ME. I feel her eyes. I can't look back.

I had this friend named Mazzy who used to talk about walking across the lake on her eighteenth birthday. We were twelve when she first brought it up. Said she'd figured out a way to do it.

We used to hang out on the roof together. Sophy would sit by the smokestack and watch us. She'd watch us for hours and never say anything or even move from her spot, playing with an old bald baby doll and a truck she loved.

Mazzy would point at the lake.

I'd listen and look at the lake and Sophy.

Mazzy moved before she got to see if lake-walking would work. I think about her a lot. More than I used to think about her when she was around.

She was the second person to know that something was wrong. My baby sister, Sophy, was the first. Kids are sensitive, I guess.

Sometimes, in the early days, I thought she was the only other person in the world who heard Them. She'd get real close to me and wouldn't take her eyes off my face. Was she listening?

The day I got home from getting my hand

bandaged, I looked in the boxes under her bed. Don't know why she took the stuff she took. I guess she just grabbed what she could.

She's stuffing pain in the boxes. She still looks at me the way she did when she was five. I think she's waiting for it to happen to her. Don't think it will, but I can't find the words to tell her. Can't speak 'em.

So I take her to the airport and stand real close to her during storms. I follow her around the city, too. I don't think she's ever seen me. I become a part of her as she watches people at the bus station or sits in Doggy's, drinking coffee. I think she needs more friends, but I don't think she'd agree. I know she wouldn't.

She's keeping me awake at night. I can only sleep when I make her disappear. I told the doctor in the emergency room the other night that my sister was making my heart hurt. Aunt Shirley handed him my medication and left the room.

Aunt Shirley's face was tear-stained when I found her in the waiting room, and it made me think that I should have told her a long time ago about Mazzy's plan to walk across Lake Erie. She could have walked across the water a long time ago . . .

I've been cutting out pictures from magazines. I'm trying to get away from people in blue clothes. It's hard. I try every single day. I think about other things.

I watch Sophy dance. She's better than I ever was.

The woman next door thinks it's a good idea for her to use the barre *in her attic, but I haven't told Sophy yet. I've been watching out for her. She makes my heart hurt, though.*

I can still picture her looking at the boy at the popcorn machine when she was four. I remember how she pressed her face to the glass and smiled at him as I turned and walked into the parking lot.

I should tell her about lake-walking, too, 'cause she was a baby on the roof when Mazzy first explained it, and that was a long time ago.

21

I T MUST BE the middle of the night when I hear Reuben's voice. Nicole is still sleeping in the bed beside mine. It's late, 'cause I don't hear the women on the street any more. A few minutes later, a door closes, and I watch from my window as Reuben drives away.

AUNT SHIRLEY tells me in the morning that Miss Onyx has had a stroke. She can't talk or move. She goes on to say that a woman like Miss Onyx shouldn't end this way – what with the life she's lived and all.

I think about Miss Onyx telling me everyone in her family had died in the Nazi death camps. She told me when she'd walked out of the camp at the end of the war, she knew that there was nothing in this world that would ever scare her again.

I go back in the bedroom to watch Nicole sleep. She whispers, wearing a blue nightgown. I lean over and kiss her head.

All I can think of are the numbers on Miss Onyx's wrist and the way her apartment smelled of peppermint the last time I was there.

I look up and it's snowing. You can never tell. The birds will just be singing their hearts out and it's spring ... Reuben said he remembers a time when snow was still in dirty piles into May. I asked him what year that was, and he said, "One year in one of my lives."

Nikki smiled at that.

MISS ONYX was asleep when I first picked up her hand and held it. She woke in a few minutes.

We'd made sure her hospital room felt like home. I put a corner of one of her blankets from home in her hand for her to feel.

Classical music played softly around us.

I talked to her for two hours.

I reminded her of last winter, when she took me to the ballet. It had been all soft light and music. Miss Onyx sat with her back straight during the whole performance. She was at dancer's attention and had a secret smile all night. I could imagine her onstage. She didn't look as if any of her dancing had been stolen from her.

I told her I thought Nikki's dancing had been stolen. She still danced, but not the way she did when I followed her through the house, wearing her shoes that were triple the size of my feet.

Lump Willow sat three seats in front of us that night. During intermission I introduced him to Miss Onyx. He was all in black, just like the woman beside him. She shimmered in the lights, and both of them bowed their heads to Miss Onyx.

Dancers' bows.

Miss Onyx, through it all, looked up from her bed into my eyes.

WHEN MISS ONYX and I had walked out of the ballet into the cold last winter, Reuben stood waiting for us at the door of his jeep.

"Did you have a good evening?"

Miss Onyx nodded and slid into the jeep. Smiling to the last.

I said, "Cold night, huh?"

Reuben looked up at the sky.

"Maybe it'll snow into May," he said.

And now it has.

22

I SIT ON THE STOOP, flipping through one of Nicole's scrapbooks. She keeps a record in it of everything she cares about.

One of Nicole's favourite songs is called "Crossroad Blues". She can sit for hours and listen to it over and over. She has a picture of the singer pasted in somewhere right next to Reuben and our daddy. She says they have a place in her soul – a place she holds on to even when everything else is slipping away. Says the place where they live is brave.

She leans over and whispers to me.

"Did you know that our daddy saved two of his friends from drowning when he was fifteen? He jumped in a creek with his boots on and pulled them out of the water. He told me that once when we were fishing. That's something, huh?"

I say, "It is," as she walks away down the sidewalk, out to the street, talking to herself.

I watch her go. When she gets about half a block away, she turns around and screams, "I'd save you, too, Sophy. I'd never let you drown."

The kids across the street play music that I recognize on garbage cans. I like the sound.

When I go back to the scrapbook, I notice that Nicole has glued a picture of me between the "Crossroads" singer and Reuben.

A LIST:

Look for summer job
Offer help to Evangaline Macon
Ask her about *barre* in attic
Visit Miss Onyx
Visit Miss Onyx
Find buy blue shorts for Nikki
Dance
Dance
Dance
No fear
Live
Live
Live

I'VE BEEN CAREFUL with the mirror lately. I don't just jump in front of it like I used to. I go slowly. Gently. I don't want to surprise it. I want to be the same as the day before. It's been working.

One morning, though, Nikki was up before me. I stood in the doorway of the bathroom and watched her press her face to the glass. It must have been cold 'cause at first she jumped. Then she relaxed and closed her eyes.

I never closed my eyes. I would search all over the mirror when I thought I might have changed in the night. I don't know what Nikki was seeing, but whatever it was, she accepted it. Her face relaxed.

I WONDER what it must feel like to walk under Lake Erie during a storm. Water rushing and filling the world.

I think it must be quiet and peaceful, like a dream I had. It was a world without sound in my dream ...

I sit on the stoop with Nikki as a storm comes closer, almost over us. The street is clear. The garbage cans are empty except for their tops. The women across the street have all gone in, the kids, too.

Nicole and I wait for the beginning. I shake only a little.

When the storm is almost on top of us, Nikki

stands up and runs into the courtyard – dancing all around. It's not a frantic dance; it welcomes me. I want to be with her. Nikki dances like she never has. Over the lightning and thunder. She dances over the rain pouring down on us. She dances over all of it. Then she stops and holds her hand out to me.

I take it.

It must be quiet under the Great Lakes. There's ships and people under there, and they don't make a sound. I don't either as I dance around the courtyard with my sister.

When the storm is right above us, and at its strongest, there's not one sound. Not even a whisper.